Toilet paper!

created by
Joshua McManus

So we are here to show you
because I bet you never knew!

Wrap it round your bum
for perfect underwear.

Or give your dear old grandad
lots of funky hair.

Try toilet paper pom-poms
strapped upon each wrist.

Or do the weekly shopping
with a toilet paper list.

You can wind it round your head
for a perfect winter's hat.

It can be a soft white carpet
when rolled out nice and flat.

Why not bungee jump with
extra toilet paper spring?

Or go up high in the sky
on a toilet paper swing?

Try a toilet paper hammock, yes!
And drift right off to sleep.

Or cover your whole body
and look like a silly sheep!

Toilet paper is a great display
when launched with perfect speed.

And also very good as a
giant long dog lead!

Toilet paper will wrap a gift,
and make it look quite smart.

Or slap it on a wall so it
becomes the perfect art!

Why not try and balance
on a toilet paper tower?

Or become a superhero with
super toilet paper power?

Dance just like a loony
in a toilet paper skirt?

Or wrapped around your knees
so falling doesn't hurt?

Toilet paper, nice and tight,
will sound just like a drum.

Wiping your bum!

available at amazon

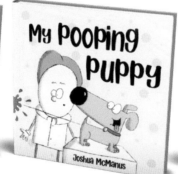

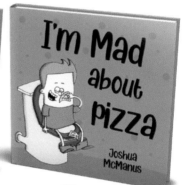

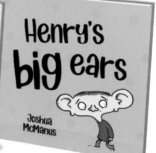

Printed in Great Britain
by Amazon

80823502R00018